Tom and Ricky

and the

Silver Buckle Mystery

Bob Wright

High Noon Books
Novato, California

Cover Design and Illustrations: Herb Heidinger

Glossary: friend, hospital, nurse, belt, family, Canada, maple

International Standard Book Number: 0-87879-340-2

. 7 6 5 4 3 2 1 0 9 8
4 3 2 1 0 9 8 7 6 5

High Noon Books
a division of ATP
20 Commercial Blvd.
Novato, California 94949

Contents

CHAPTER 1

A Mystery to Clear Up

Ricky got off his bike. He locked it. Then he took a big bag off the back of the bike. The bag was filled with things. Everything in the bag was for his friend, Tom.

"So this is the hospital he's in," Ricky said.

Ricky had been to the hospital just one time. He knew where the front door was. But he wasn't sure where Tom was. It seemed like a big place to him. He went in the front door. Then he stopped.

1

"Now what do I do? I better ask what room Tom is in," he said.

He saw a nurse. She looked at him. She seemed to know he needed help.

"Are you looking for someone?" she asked.

"I have a friend here. I'm looking for him. Do you know what room he is in?" Ricky asked.

"What's your friend's name?" the nurse asked.

"Tom," Ricky answered.

"Tom? Sure, I know Tom. I think all the nurses know Tom. Everyone here likes him. You must be Ricky," she said.

"How do you know who I am?" Ricky asked.

"Tom has told us a lot about you and him," she said.

"How is his leg?" Ricky asked.

"Everyone here likes him. You must be Ricky."

"Tom is doing just fine. I think he might be going home in a day or two," she said.

"What's your name?" Ricky asked.

"I'm Mary. I'm the nurse on Tom's floor here at the hospital," Mary said.

"This is a big place. Can you tell me how to get to Tom's room?" Ricky asked.

"I'll take you there. I have to go that way," Mary said.

Ricky walked with Mary. There were a lot of people walking around the hospital. He was glad she was taking him to Tom's room. That way he would get there faster.

"How did Tom hurt his arm and leg?" Mary asked.

"Didn't he tell you?" Ricky asked.

"Well, he just said he fell off his bike," Mary said.

"We both have dirt bikes. Tom was trying to go over a small hill. He jumped his bike too much. My dog, Patches, got in front of him. He wanted to miss Patches and fell off," Ricky said.

"Tom likes to talk. He has told us that you and he like to clear up mysteries," Mary said.

Ricky didn't know what to say. "We've helped our friend Sergeant Collins clear up some mysteries," he said.

"Is Sergeant Collins your friend, too? I know him very well. He has helped us here at the hospital," Mary said.

Ricky liked Mary. He was glad she knew Sergeant Collins, too.

"We have a mystery here at the hospital," Mary said.

"A mystery? Here at the hospital?" Ricky asked.

"Yes. I'll tell you about it later. Here's Tom's room. Does he know you are coming?" Mary asked.

"No," Ricky answered.

"Well, I think he's going to be happy to see you," Mary said.

CHAPTER 2

A Busted Leg

Ricky looked in the room. Tom was the only one in it. Tom didn't see or hear Ricky. Tom was looking at TV. Then Tom looked over at the door.

"Ricky! Boy, am I glad to see you," Tom called.

"How are you doing?" Ricky asked.

"My leg is getting better. That fall was bad. How is Patches?" Tom asked.

"Patches is fine," Ricky said.

"What's in that bag?" Tom asked.

"Oh, not too much," Ricky answered.

"Come on. Let me see," Tom said.

Ricky took the bag over to Tom.

Tom let everything fall out onto the bed. He could use just one arm but he didn't care. There were games, cards, and comic books.

"Just what I need. I was getting tired of all that TV! Now I have some things to do. Thanks, Ricky," Tom said.

"Tom, I know you hurt your leg, but what about your arm?" Ricky asked.

"Oh, that. I busted my leg a lot and my arm a little. The arm is going to be better right away. The leg will take a little longer," Tom said.

"That leg does look bad. How long will it take to walk on it? When will you get to go home?" Ricky asked.

"As soon as my arm is better. That will be in a day or two. I will be able to get around even though my leg will still be getting better," Tom said.

"Mary said you have been talking about us," Ricky said.

"I sure have. I like the nurses here. I told them about some of the mysteries we helped clear up," Tom said.

"Mary said she has a mystery that we can help clear up," Ricky said.

"She told me that, too," Tom said.

"Do you know what she was talking about?" Ricky asked.

"No. All she told me was that there was a mystery. Then she said maybe we could help out," Tom said.

"Mary knows Sergeant Collins," Ricky said.

"That's what she told me," Tom said.

"Do you think he has something to do with the mystery?" Ricky asked.

Just then Mary walked into the room. "How are you two doing?" she asked.

"We were talking about the hospital mystery," Tom said.

"I think you both need a good mystery to work on," Mary said

"Well, tell us what the mystery is," Ricky said.

"I won't have to tell you very much," she said.

"Then how can we help clear it up?" Tom asked.

"This is one mystery you are going to meet," she said.

"Meet a mystery?" Ricky asked.

"What's this all about?" Tom asked.

"I told you it was a mystery," she said.

"Tell us a little more," Tom said.

"I won't have to. Here comes the mystery right now," she said.

CHAPTER 3

The Mystery Boy

A mystery coming down the hall? What was this all about? Tom and Ricky didn't know what was going on.

"What's out in the hall?" Tom asked.

"The mystery boy," Mary said.

"Mary, is this some kind of a game?" Ricky asked.

"No, it is a mystery. We need help on this one," she said.

"I hope we can help you, Mary," Tom said.

12

"The mystery boy is going to stay in this room with you, Tom. That's how we're going to start to clear up the mystery," Mary said.

The wheel chair was being pushed by their friend, Sergeant Collins.

Just then a little boy came into the room. He was in a wheel chair. Tom's eyes opened wide. So did Ricky's. The wheel chair was being pushed by their friend, Sergeant Collins.

"What are you doing here?" Tom asked.

"I heard about your leg and arm. You're my friend so I came to see you. But I have a new case to clear up," Sergeant Collins said.

Sergeant Collins was standing by the little boy in the wheel chair. The boy looked like he might be about seven years old.

The little boy didn't say anything. He just looked at Tom and Ricky.

"Tell us about the new case," Ricky said.

The Sergeant looked at the little boy. "Well,

my new case and this little boy are the same thing," Sergeant Collins said.

"What do you mean?" Tom asked.

"How could they be the same thing?" Ricky asked.

Sergeant Collins looked over at Mary. "You know all about it, Mary. Will you tell them the story?"

"OK. I'll be happy to tell you all about it. But first I want you to meet Billy," Mary said.

"Mary, I thought you said this was the mystery boy," Tom said.

"I did say that. You see, we don't know Billy's real name," Mary said.

They all looked at Mary.

"What? Why are you calling him Billy?" Ricky asked.

"He needed a name," Mary said.

Mary looked at Billy. "Billy, this is Tom and this is Ricky," she said.

Billy looked at Tom and Ricky. "Hi," he said to them.

"Mary, what is all this about?" Tom asked.

"Do you boys ever forget anything?" Mary asked.

"All the time," Tom said.

"Me, too," Ricky said.

"We all do that. But then it comes back. Right?" she asked.

"That's right," Tom said.

"Well, sometimes people forget for a long time. They forget a lot of things. They forget who they are, their name, and where they live. But they don't forget how to talk," Mary said.

"You mean that Billy doesn't know his own name or the name of his mother and father or where he lives?" Tom asked.

"That's right," Mary said.

"Now I see why you said you had a mystery to clear up," Ricky said.

"This is going to be a hard one," Tom said.

"Did Billy forget how to walk?" Ricky asked.

"Oh, no. He can still walk," Mary said.

"Then why is he in the wheel chair?" Ricky asked.

"He is a little hurt. Sergeant Collins will tell you about that," Mary said.

Billy looked at Mary. Then he got up out of the wheel chair and walked over to see Tom. He looked at Tom's arm and leg.

"See my leg. I can't use it right now. I'll use my arm again in one or two days," Tom said to Billy.

Tom looked up at Sergeant Collins. "Can you tell us more about Billy?" he asked.

"How did he get here to the hospital?" Ricky asked.

Billy stayed by Tom's bed. He kept looking at Tom's arm and leg.

"That's a nice buckle," Tom said.

18

"Billy was found standing by the side of Front Street. He was all alone. No one knows who he is or where he is from. That is why he was taken here to the hospital. Maybe he can be helped here," Sergeant Collins said.

"So we don't know anything about Billy," Ricky said.

All of a sudden Tom called out, "Yes we do! We know his name. We know his name is Ray Decker!"

"What? How do you know that?" Sergeant Collins said.

CHAPTER 4

The Silver Buckle

Everyone looked at Tom. How could he know Billy's real name? The little boy looked at Tom. He wasn't sure what his real name was.

"Tom, how do you know his real name is Ray Decker?" Ricky asked.

"Look at his belt! Look at the buckle on his belt," Tom called out.

Sergeant Collins walked over to the little boy. "Come here. Let me see your belt and that buckle," he said.

The little boy let Sergeant Collins look at the buckle on his belt.

"How about that!" Sergeant Collins said.

"Look at his belt! Look at the buckle on his belt."

"Let me see it," Ricky said.

The little boy took off his belt and gave it to Ricky.

Ricky looked at the buckle. He wanted to know how Tom knew the little boy's real name.

"I see it! I see it!" Ricky said.

Right there on the buckle were the letters "R A Y D E C K E R."

"That's how you knew his name. You have good eyes!" Sergeant Collins said.

Mary walked over and looked at the buckle.

"There it was. All the time his name was there but we just didn't see it," Mary said.

Sergeant Collins looked at the buckle, "This looks like silver, but it couldn't be."

"Where would a little boy get a real silver buckle with his name on it?" Tom asked.

Mary looked at the little boy. "I'll tell everyone here what your name is, Ray," she said.

Ray looked up at her. He still didn't know what was going on.

"Ray, you get to stay in this room with Tom. Would you like that?" Mary asked.

"I sure would," Ray said.

"We have to keep you here at the hospital," Mary said.

"Why is that?" Tom asked.

"We have to clear up all of this mystery," Sergeant Collins said.

"But we know his name," Tom said.

"Yes, but we don't know where he lives. We have to find out more about Ray. We have to find his family," the Sergeant said.

Ricky looked at Ray. "Do you think your name is Ray? Does it sound right to you?"

"I think that's my name. I'm not sure," Ray answered.

Then Mary said, "I have to go now. But I'll be back."

"I have to go, too. I'm going to come back. But I want to see if there are any Deckers living near here," Sergeant Collins said.

"You know what?" Ricky said.

"What?" Ray answered.

"I think you must be very rich," Ricky said.

"Why do you say that?" Tom asked.

"I think that buckle is all silver," Ricky answered.

"All silver!" Tom said.

"And look. Do you see something in back of Ray's name?" Ricky asked.

"Yes, I do. There is something on that buckle," Tom said.

"It looks like a leaf, doesn't it?" Ricky said.

"It sure does," Tom said.

"Do you think the leaf means something?" Ricky asked.

"It has to mean something. That buckle had to be made just for Ray. His name is on it. It is silver," Tom said.

CHAPTER 5

The Maple Leaf

Ricky kept on looking at the silver buckle. He wanted to know what the leaf might mean. He knew it had to mean something.

Just then Sergeant Collins walked into the room.

"What did you find out? Are there any Deckers living in town?" Tom called out.

"Yes, there are," Sergeant Collins said.

He sat down in the wheel chair.

"Ray, did you hear that?" Tom said.

"But wait. There is just one family. And they don't know anyone named Ray," Sergeant Collins said.

"Oh, no," Ricky said. He looked over at Ray.

Ray didn't say anything. He just looked at Sergeant Collins.

"Don't worry, Ray. We will find your family," Ricky said.

"Did you find out more?" Tom asked.

"Well, yes, I did. The Mr. Decker who lives here said he thinks there might be some Deckers living in Canada. He is not sure. He knew them a long, long time ago," Sergeant Collins said.

"In Canada?" Tom asked.

"That's a long way from here," Ricky said.

Sergeant Collins started to laugh.

Everyone looked at him.

"What's so funny?" Ricky asked.

"Well, Mr. Decker who lives here is very old. But he said he would like to know the Deckers who live in Canada. He said they are very rich," Sergeant Collins said.

Just then Mary walked into the room. "Who's rich?" she asked.

"Some people who live in Canada," Sergeant Collins answered.

"Tom and I think that Ray might be very rich, too," Ricky said.

"Why is that?" Mary asked.

"That buckle on Ray's belt is real silver. It is all silver," Ricky answered.

Mary took the buckle. "Let me see that. I know a little about silver. Yes, I would say that this is all silver," she said.

"Take a close look at the buckle, Mary," Tom said.

"What do you see on it?" Ricky asked.

"You boys do like to clear up mysteries. Well, I see Ray's name. I see something in back of his name," she said.

"Do you think it could be a leaf?" Ricky asked.

Mary looked at the buckle again. "Why, yes, it is. It is a leaf."

"Now I have to see the buckle. Give it to me," Sergeant Collins said.

Mary gave him the silver buckle.

"This is a leaf. It's a maple leaf!" Sergeant Collins said.

"What could that mean? Why is it there with Ray's name?" Tom asked.

"Wait! Doesn't the maple leaf stand for Canada?" Ricky said.

"It sure does. It is on the flag of Canada," Mary answered.

No one said anything.

Then Ricky said, "That might mean that Ray is from Canada!"

"But how did he get here?" Tom asked.

"I'm going to call Canada. I'm going to ask the police there if someone named Ray Decker is missing," Sergeant Collins said. Then he left.

"I almost forgot why I came back up here," Mary said.

"What's that?" Ricky asked.

"There's a man here. He wants to see Ray. He says he is his father," Mary said.

"Your father, Ray. Your father is here," Tom called out.

"It looks like our mystery is cleared up," Ricky said.

"I'll get him," Mary said.

CHAPTER 6

The Man in the Dark Coat

Mary came back in the room. The man was big. He had on a dark coat. The coat was old and dirty. He looked mad.

"Where is my boy?" he asked.

Then the man saw Ray. He walked over to him. Ray didn't say anything. He just looked at the man.

"Did you forget your father?" the man asked.

"Are you my father?" Ray asked.

"You mean you forgot me, too?" the man asked.

Ray still didn't say anything.

The man was big. He wore a dark coat. The coat was old and dirty.

Ricky talked to Tom so no one could hear them. "You know what?" Tom said.

"What?" Ricky answered.

"I don't think Ray is very rich," Tom said.

"Why do you think that?" Ricky asked.

"Rich people have good coats. That man's coat is all dirty," Tom said.

"Look at Ray and that man. They don't even look alike," Ricky said.

"That's right. Ray doesn't even look like his father."

The man and Mary were talking.

All of a sudden the man yelled at Mary. "What do you mean? Why can't I take my son out of the hospital? I am his father!"

"I'm sorry. You can't do that. You can not take him out," Mary said.

"Just tell me why," he yelled.

"Ray just can't leave. We have to make sure he is OK," Mary answered.

"You can't tell me what to do. That kid is my son. And I'm taking him with me," he yelled at Mary.

Then the man looked at Ray. "You want to go with me, don't you?" he asked.

"No, I don't," Ray said.

"Well, you are going to. Right now," he yelled at Ray.

"Why don't you want to go, Ray?" Tom asked.

"I don't like him," Ray answered.

"Don't like me? Don't like your father?" the man yelled.

Now the man was mad. He grabbed the belt and Ray. Then he said, "Come on. Right now."

"You are not taking Ray from the hospital," Mary said.

"Is that so?" the man said.

"That's so," Mary said.

The man pulled a gun out of his coat. "Stay where you are. Don't move. I'm taking this kid with me."

CHAPTER 7

The Mystery Is Cleared Up

No one moved. The man had a gun. Mary didn't know what to do. She wanted to help Ray. Tom and Ricky didn't say anything.

Then they all heard, "OK, Mr. Rack. Put that gun down. Drop that belt."

It was Sergeant Collins. He had said he would be back.

The man didn't move. He didn't know who was in back of him.

Tom yelled out, "Sergeant Collins!"

Mr. Rack dropped the gun and the belt.

"Sit down. Don't move," Sergeant Collins

said.

Then they all heard, "OK, Mr. Rack. Put that gun
down. Drop that belt."

Mr. Rack saw Sergeant Collins's gun. He sat down in the wheel chair.

"Look, Sergeant. I'm just here to get my son. All I want to do is take him home," Mr. Rack said.

"He's not your son," Sergeant Collins said.

The man didn't say anything.

"How did you know his name is Mr. Rack?" Tom asked.

"I called the police in Canada. Ray's family is very, very rich. Ray was taken away from his family ten days ago. The police in Canada have been looking for Ray," Sergeant Collins said.

"But why did Ray forget who he is?" Tom asked.

"I'll tell you. Here's what it is all about," Sergeant Collins said.

Mr. Rack didn't move. He just sat in the wheel chair.

"Mr. Rack knew the police in Canada were after him. He left Canada with Ray. He didn't think the police would come to our small town looking for him," Sergeant Collins said.

"Tom and Ricky did help. It was good that Ray had that silver buckle," Mary said.

"That's right. Without that silver buckle we would not have called the police in Canada," Sergeant Collins said.

"But what about Ray? Why did he forget everything?" Ricky asked.

"Ray was in Mr. Rack's car. Mr. Rack hit a pole near here. His car went off the road. He hit his head. Then he passed out for a long time," Sergeant Collins said.

Everyone looked at Mr. Rack. He put his hand over a bump on his head. But everyone could see the bump.

Sergeant Collins went on. "Ray bumped his head, too. But he didn't pass out. He got out of the car and walked up to the road. He didn't see anything so he kept on walking."

"How did he get here to the hospital?" Ricky asked.

"How did he know where the hospital was?" Tom asked.

"A man saw him all alone at night on Front Street. The man stopped his car. He asked Ray where he lived. Ray didn't know. Then the man asked his name. He didn't know. Ray didn't know anything. So the man took him here," Sergeant Collins said.

Everyone looked at Ray.

All of a sudden Ray started to talk. "That's right! That's right! Now I know. I know everything. It's all coming back. My name is Ray Decker. I live in Banks, Canada. My dad's name is Ed. My mother's name is Mary," he yelled.

"Mary! Just like my name," Mary said.

"That's right," Ray yelled. He was happy. He knew who he was.

Then Sergeant Collins looked at Mr. Rack. "Well, we can all see that you are not Ray's dad. You took Ray from Canada. You wanted Mr. and Mrs. Decker to give you money for Ray. I think it's time for me to take you in," Sergeant Collins said.

Mr. Rack got up. He went with Sergeant Collins.

"Can I call my mom and dad?" Ray asked.

"You sure can," Mary said.

Then Mary looked at Tom and Ricky. "Maybe Mr. Rack would have taken Ray. You cleared up this mystery when you saw Ray's name and the maple leaf on the silver buckle," she said.

Ray looked at Tom and Ricky. "Will you come and stay with me in Canada?" he asked.

"Maybe one day soon we can," Ricky said.

"Canada is a long way from here. It would cost a lot of money to go there," Tom said.

"Don't worry. My mom and dad are rich. I know they will pay for everything," Ray said.

Then Mary took Ray to call his mom and dad.

"What a mystery this has been," Tom said.

"It sure has been. Just don't fall off your bike any more," Ricky said.

"Tell that to Patches," Tom laughed.